Cont

Chapter 1
Dragons in the Sky

They came at dawn.

The sky was as red as blood and the clouds were ragged and black. The sea was as dark and oily-smooth as a monk's ink. The sails were dirty, dark smudges on the crimson sky.

I know this because my sister, Emma, saw them before anyone.

Emma sat on the cliff top shivering under her brown woollen cloak, which was the colour of autumn leaves. She knew she should run to the village and warn the people. She should hammer at the monastery door and tell the monks to ring the bell. Tell them to ring out three booming clangs from the tower bell. The sound of that bell was the message they dreaded.

"The Vikings are back!"

But Emma couldn't move for a while. She couldn't take her eyes off the sword-sharp vessels that slid over the dark water. The black clouds split and the jagged red sky between them looked like a monstrous dragon.

Emma watched as the leather sails slid down the masts and the heavy oars were lowered into the water. Three dozen men on each ship pulled powerfully on their oars towards the beach. She could make out the dragon's head on the prows of the ships. A

small figure clung to the steering oar at the back of one.

"They cut the throats of the old and they carry away the young to be their slaves," Emma said to herself. "I think I'd rather have my throat cut."

She knew she should run now and give the monks in the monastery a chance to escape. But her eyes were fixed on the ship that cut through the water like a swallow through the air.

At the very last moment, the young boy at the ship's helm gave a cry. And then the men raised their oars into the air and the ships slid onto the pebbled beach with a crunch.

Emma took one last look and saw the men fixing their shields onto their arms. She wriggled backwards till she was below the brow of the cliff.

She snatched at the bridle of the white pony that was grazing there, flung herself onto its back and kicked it hard with her heels. The startled animal jumped forward and Emma had to hang on hard to its mane as it raced down the slope towards the stone walls of the monastery by the river. Emma's dark hair came unpinned and it lashed at her face as she hurtled down the slope.

Smoke drifted up from the kitchens where Emma knew they'd be cooking the tasteless porridge the monks ate for breakfast every day. She also knew that very soon smoke and flames would be rising from the burning monastery.

She threw herself down from the pony and stumbled to the great oak gate of the monastery. She lifted the iron knocker and smashed it onto the wood again and again. After a long time a small door set into the main gate swung open and a thin old monk stood there. He scowled at her. His mouth was turned down in a sour frown.

"So it's you, Emma," he said. "I thought you were on your way home to Durham. You left at dawn ..."

"Listen, Edmund. Vikings!" Emma said, panting. "The Vikings are coming. I got to the cliff path and I saw them! The Vikings are coming to steal and kill!"

The monk folded his arms and blocked her way. "You've been dreaming of your brother Symeon's tales again," he said. "You're as bad as him. There are no Vikings."

Emma's green eyes glared at him. "I hope they cut your throat first, Edmund – then you'll be sorry."

"How can I be sorry if my throat has been cut?" the monk sneered.

"You'll be sorry when ... when you see the sword swing down!" Emma snapped.

"My God will be with me."

"Then I hope for your sake that he's wearing armour," she said.

Chapter 2
The Broken Bell

Emma stood shivering at the gate to the monastery. "Are you going to let me in?" she asked Edmund.

"Not while the monks are having breakfast," the old gate-keeper replied. "They must eat in peace."

Emma knew it was no use trying to argue with this old man. "Be careful!" she said, pointing at a spot above his head. "That spider is just about to land on your bald spot!"

As the old man looked up, Emma slipped past him. He called after her, but he would never catch her. They say the devil can take the shape of a hare. And I swear that Emma was a devil and she could run like a hare.

Emma sped along the stone paths and into the refectory where we were eating in silence. She flung open the door. The only sound was the soft clack of our wooden spoons on wooden bowls.

Then there was the soft sound of a young monk groaning. That young monk was me. My sister Emma was going to make me feel ashamed of her – again.

"The Vikings are coming!" she cried. "Collect up your gold and hide it away. Then run for your lives."

Our leader, the abbot, rose to his feet, smiling. Everyone was shocked when he spoke. No one *ever* spoke at meals. God did not allow it.

"Emma, child," the abbot said and wiped his greasy hands on his woollen robe. "You have had a dream. Vikings who robbed and killed are raiders from the past. There are no Vikings any more."

"I SAW them!" Emma shouted.

The abbot turned to me. "Take your sister out and see that she gets safely on the road to Durham, will you, Symeon?" he said.

"Yes, abbot," I muttered. Even in the cold refectory, I was burning with shame. I grabbed my sister by the arm and dragged her to the door.

But Emma broke free and called over her shoulder, "Let the Vikings kill you. But I'm going to save the people of the village."

Then she stamped her boot on my toe and, as I fell back, she ran. I chased her back to the main gate. I could see she wasn't running to the village but to the tall stone tower at the edge of the wood. The bell tower.

Emma was going to ring the bell with three single strokes. That was the signal that said – "Vikings!"

Everyone would panic. Men would run from the fields, driving their cattle and sheep to safety. Women would snatch their children and race to hide in the woods. Everyone would rush to bury their coins and anything else of any value.

But if after all that there was no Viking raid ... then they would want to give the person who had rung the bell a good beating.

12

Emma dashed across the grass. Sheep scattered out of her way. She got to the door of the tower a moment before me. She slammed the door against my knee and ran up the wooden stairs to the top.

I limped after her. My knee hurt. I prayed that God would make her slip and break her nasty neck. But God let me down.

Emma reached the top of the tower, panting and red-faced. She grabbed the bell, pulled it to her and looked across the room at me.

She let the bell swing towards me. At that moment two things happened. I glanced over her shoulder and looked through the window at the top of the tower. Something was moving out there. I saw a band of hard-faced, well-armed men marching over the hill towards the monastery and the village.

The second thing that happened was
that the bell creaked on its beam and swung
towards me ... without a sound.

Someone had taken the clapper out of the
bell. A traitor had broken it so that there could
be no warning signal.

I knew then that we were beaten.

Chapter 3
The Traitor at the Gate

Emma looked at me and her mouth fell open. "We've been betrayed," she whispered.

The bell creaked gently and slowed to a stop.

Soon we would hear the tramp of the Vikings' feet. I wondered how it would feel to be hacked down.

But Emma did not plan to become a Viking slave. She grabbed my woollen robe and dragged me down to the floor. "Stay away from the windows," she said. "Then they won't see us."

"What's the point?" I asked.

"Don't you see? We can stay here till evening. Then when it's dark we can make a run for York and fetch the Norman soldiers."

"The Vikings will find us long before then," I told her. "They'll kill me and put you in chains."

"Bolt the door," Emma said.

"What?"

"Run down the stairs and bolt the door," she ordered.

I shook my head but did what I was told. Then I climbed back up the stairs to the bell room at the top.

I could hear cries of fear from the villagers. I raised my eyes above the window sill and looked down. The Vikings were pushing the villagers back into their houses, slapping some with the sides of their swords, but not stabbing or chopping.

The Vikings were herding crying children like sheep. They were pushing angry men with their round Viking shields. But no battle-axe was raised – no blood flowed.

A fat Viking stood and shouted orders. When he was sure the villagers were safe in their houses, he turned to the monastery.

I sighed. My poor brother monks. They would be beaten and robbed. I watched as the fat Viking leader strode up to the monastery gate. He used the end of his sword to hammer at it. Our bell tower was only 20 paces away, so I could hear everything that went on.

I knew they would be able to hear us if we clattered over the wooden floor of the bell tower. So we crept around.

I waited for old Edmund to open the gate. Emma had taken off her riding boots and she walked on tip-toes to my side. We watched the gate swing open.

Emma gasped.

"Shhhh!" I hissed.

"But it's ..."

"Shhhh! I know," I said, looking down at the fat man who now stood at the gate. "It's the abbot himself."

"What a brave man," Emma murmured, "to face the Vikings alone."

It was a surprise to see the abbot answer the knock at the gate. But what happened next was an even bigger surprise.

The abbot opened his fat arms wide. He grinned and stepped forward. The Viking leader lowered his sword and stretched out his arms too. The two men hugged one another. I heard the abbot cry, "Earl Hakkon, my friend! Welcome! A thousand welcomes!"

I looked at Emma. "Not a brave man," I said.

"No," she agreed. "A traitor. The most evil traitor that ever lived."

Chapter 4
Escape from the Tower

The abbot threw open both gates and 50 of the Viking raiders poured into the monastery. Another dozen stayed outside to watch over the villagers in their homes.

"The harvest was gathered just a few weeks ago. There is plenty of food for them," I said.

"But what do the Vikings want? It doesn't look as if they've come to rob the monastery," Emma said.

I needed to think about that. I sat on the floor with my back against the wooden wall. "Maybe they want a better prize. A richer prize. Maybe they want to raid York."

Emma nodded. "You aren't so stupid after all, brother," she said.

"And you were right when you tried to warn us," I said with a sigh. "We should have listened to you."

Emma shook her head. "It would have made no difference," she said.

"It would," I argued. "We'd have had time to get to York and warn the Norman army. Now the villagers are trapped in their homes and we are stuck in this bell tower."

"We will just have to wait until dark," Emma sighed. "The Vikings will be watching the houses but not this tower. Not when they know the bell has been broken. We can do it, Symeon. We can save England."

That was the plan. We sat on the floor and talked. The Normans had invaded the north of England back in 1067. They were harsh rulers, but no worse than some of our own Saxon lords who ruled the country before they came. At least the Normans brought peace.

Some Saxon lords, like our own father, made peace with the Normans and were able to keep their land. Father even hoped to marry Emma off to a Norman when she was old enough at 13. I felt sorry for the man who married her. Not even the worst of the Normans deserved to be married to my sister.

Since the Normans came, the monasteries had grown richer – and our abbot had grown fatter. So why had he turned against our Norman masters? Why had he become a traitor? He was a Saxon.

The hours went by. The sun rose high in the sky. We grew hungry and thirsty, but I was used to fasting in the monastery. I would go for two days with nothing more than a little water. The hunger hurt Emma's greedy belly more than mine.

"If we can save England," I said, "then a bit of hunger will be worth it."

"I am so hungry I could cut off your leg and eat it," my sweet sister said. She touched the knife she kept at her belt and licked her lips.

I was going to tell her I'd cut off her hair if she didn't behave. Then we heard a noise below. We peered out of the window. The Vikings were bustling about. They had taken all the horses, oxen and farm carts from the village and had put them in a line outside the monastery door. We watched them load sacks of corn, barrels of wine and bags of meat onto the wagons.

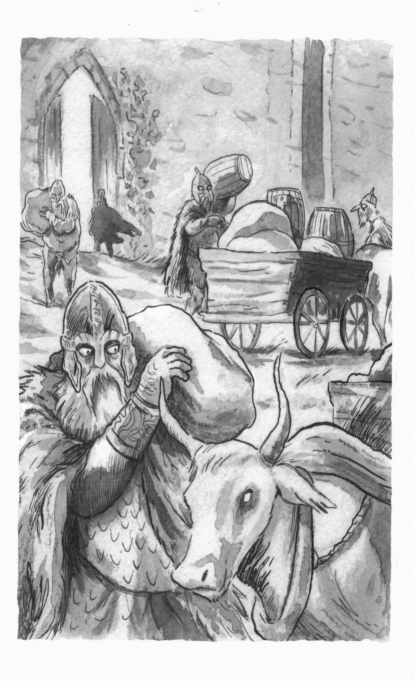

"They are taking supplies for the battles ahead," I said. "They needed to stop here for food and wagons. They can't carry much on their boats."

Emma frowned. "It looks as if they're leaving right now. If we wait till dark we'll be too late," she said angrily. "We need another plan."

"We could make a run for it now," I said. "The Vikings are loaded down with weapons. We could be far along the woodland trail before they could catch us."

Emma nodded. "Go on, then," she said.

"Aren't you coming?" I asked.

"No," said Emma.

"Scared?"

"No. Sensible. I can run faster than a Viking with his sword and shield. But I can't run faster than the Viking arrows. See, dear brother?" she said and nodded towards the men who guarded the village. They all carried powerful bows and arrows.

I muttered a prayer. I asked God to strike my sister dumb. God let me down again. "Have you got a better idea?" I snapped.

"Yes."

"So? What is it?" I asked.

She smiled sweetly. "The door to the tower faces the monastery. As soon as we step out we will be spotted," she said.

"You're right," I admitted.

"So let's leave the tower at the back," she said.

"There is no back door," I told her.

"No, we'll have to climb out of the window at the top of the tower," Emma said.

I laughed. "It is as high as four men," I told her. "We'd break our legs."

She waved a finger under my nose just to annoy me more. "Not if we used a rope," she said.

"Oh," I gasped. "I suppose you want me to run across to the monastery and get you a rope?"

"No, dear brother," she said. "There's no need. I have a rope."

"Where?"

Emma pointed to the rope that was tied to the bell. It went down through a hole in the floor to the room below.

"Why didn't I think of that?" I muttered.

"Because you're not as clever as me, dear brother." Emma smiled. "Poor Simple Symeon."

"Please, God," I prayed, "let the Vikings catch my horrid sister and take her away as a slave."

But God was going to let me down ... again.

Chapter 5
The Last Guard

The Vikings at the monastery gate were almost ready to leave. They were too busy loading their weapons onto the last wagon to take much notice of us.

"Good luck, Hakkon," the abbot said and he slapped the fat Viking leader on the back of his greasy leather jerkin.

Emma and I worked hard with her small knife to cut the rope from the beam and then tie it to the window frame. No one was watching as we dropped the rope to the ground at the back of the tower. I climbed down first, then waited for Emma to follow. If she slipped I would be able to catch her ... or drop her.

No one saw us as we fell into the long grass, panting a little.

The road to York stretched away to the south-west towards the afternoon sun. The Viking wagons were clattering down the trail. Guards walked at either side of the road to look out for spies ... spies like us.

"We're too late," I said. "We can't travel faster than them. We'll never overtake them now. Even if we got close, we'd never be able to get past the guards."

"You're right. We need another plan," Emma said.

I closed my eyes and groaned. "Do you have an idea?"

"How did you guess? Don't you know what it is, Simple Symeon?"

"Just tell me," I said. "How can we get to York before the Vikings?"

"We can't," she said. "We would waste time trying to go south. Let's go north. The road is open. Let's go to Durham. We can warn the Normans in Durham and they can send soldiers to help their friends in York."

I looked at the Viking warriors trooping off into the distance. The villagers were still too scared to leave their houses, even though the last of the guards had gone.

Emma and I rose from the grass and hurried across to the road that ran up the coast. It climbed the hill towards the sea shore.

The Viking ships had been pulled up onto the beach below us.

"There's just one boy left to guard the ships," Emma said as we hurried past. There was a small figure huddled in the stern of the boat. He seemed to be asleep.

We climbed the cliff path and turned inland into the woods towards Durham. The wind was chilly now in the shadow of the trees. Birds called to warn one another that there were strangers in the wood. There was no one to warn us.

My legs were weak and I wasn't sure I could walk as far as Durham. "I'll gather berries and nuts," Emma said. But it was water I needed most.

I stepped off the path and found a small, dark pool. I made my hand into a cup and scooped up the sour water. I splashed some on my face.

"The water isn't sweet but it will do, Emma," I said.

I looked around. Emma was gone. She must have left the path to look for berries in the forest. Then I saw the movement of her cloak as she came out from behind an old oak tree. A Viking boy had his left hand over her mouth and with his right hand he held a knife at her throat. Even my brave sister Emma had fear in her eyes.

The boy spoke poor Saxon, but I understood what he was saying. "You will not be going to warn the Normans," he said. "Come back with me to the monastery or I will cut the girl's throat."

I nodded silently and led the way back to the village.

Chapter 6
Prisoners in the Tower

"I am Ragnar – a Viking warrior," the boy said. "I saw you in the tower and waited for you to come out. I am the best lord my war-band has ever had," he boasted.

"We saw you in the ship," I said. "You were asleep."

"You saw a bundle of clothes wrapped around a sack of food," he laughed. "I tricked you. I was in the wood. I followed you from the moment you left the tower."

"What will we do when we get back to the village?" I asked.

"We will go to your tower," he said. "It's a good place to spend the night. I will be safe there until the warriors return from York."

Ragnar had tied Emma's hands behind her back and he held the end of the leather rope.

"What if you fall asleep and we escape?" Emma asked.

"It will be too dark for you to find your way to Durham by then. And it will be too late to save York," he told her.

"What if you fall asleep and we kill you?" Emma said angrily.

"Try it." He smiled.

I took a step forward. There was a choking cry from the top of the stairs. When I moved forward the rope went tight round Emma's neck. I stepped back. The rope went slack and she gasped for air. The Viking nodded.

"If you try to escape in the night I will know," he said. "And I will push the girl down the stairs till she chokes on the rope. You see?"

I nodded. Then I spoke fast in Norman French to Emma – I was sure Ragnar could not understand us. "Well, Emma? Have you any good ideas this time?" I said.

"None," she muttered sadly.

Ragnar walked across to her and placed a hand in the middle of her back. "Do not speak Norman," he said to me. "In fact, do not say another word before morning or I will push her down the stairs – at least, I will push her as far as she can go before the rope round her neck stops her. Now sleep."

It was not easy to sleep after that. But, in the darkest hours, I fell asleep at last.

Chapter 7
The Last Viking

I awoke when the cock crowed the next morning. I was stiff and cold and starving. Ragnar and Emma were already awake. The young Viking opened a bag on his belt and shared some bread and cheese with us.

Ragnar untied the ropes and led us to the window that faced south. The morning air was still and clear. Smoke was rising into the air many miles away.

"York is burning," Ragnar said.

"How will you get there to share the loot?" Emma asked. "Your friends will forget you," she said.

Ragnar shook his head. "They will be back for the boats," he told her. "A small crew will sail back to Denmark and we will return with an even greater army. Soon all of England will be free."

Emma laughed. "Free? I thought you were here to make us slaves!"

Ragnar looked puzzled. "No. You are ruled by the Normans. We are here to help the Saxon rebels. We will set you free."

"We don't want to be free!" Emma cried. "The Normans brought us peace. You Vikings have brought us endless war. Go away and leave us alone."

Ragnar looked lost. He looked at me.

"Sorry, Ragnar," I said. "We fought the Normans and we lost. But they are better rulers than the Vikings."

He turned to the window. "It is too late," he said and stretched out an arm. He was pointing at a cloud of dust. Horses were heading towards us. "We have captured York. Now we can set the rest of England free."

He ran down the stairs and out of the door. The horsemen clattered into the centre of the village and split into groups. One party rode to the sea shore and another went straight to the monastery door.

The villagers cheered. Ragnar clutched at my arm and I had to hold him to stop him from falling to the ground. "Normans," he whispered.

We could see that those riders in helmets and chain-mail were Normans. Their captain jumped to the ground and gave orders. Four men marched into the monastery and came out, dragging the abbot between them. The abbot was thrown across a horse and led away towards York.

Emma gave a small cheer. "Serves the traitor right."

The captain of the Norman soldiers looked across at us. "He helped the Viking raiders," he said.

"I know." I nodded.

"We defeated them outside the gates of York. Now we are here to finish them off."

"Good," Emma said. She turned to Ragnar, who wasn't sure what was happening. He didn't speak Norman French.

"The Vikings will have left a guard by the ships," the captain went on. "Once we have killed him then that will be the last Viking gone."

Emma opened her mouth to say something, but I got in first. "I was on the hill top early this morning," I said. "I saw a guard on their ship."

"So, young monk, can you tell me what this guard looked like?" the captain asked.

"He was an old man," I said.

"What?" Emma looked amazed at my lie.

"He saw me and he thought I was an enemy," I said. "He ran away on the road to the north," I added.

The captain shook his head. "He's not that important," he said. He turned to climb back on his horse. He saw Ragnar staring. The captain noticed the sea boots and the sword belt. "Who's this?" he asked.

"It's ..." Emma began.

"It's my cousin," I cut in. "From the north. He's a fisherman – he doesn't speak Norman."

"He should learn – we are here to stay," the captain said.

"I know," I said.

"What is he doing here?" the captain asked.

"He's come to join me at the monastery. He wants to be a monk," I said.

The captain nodded, climbed on his horse and rode off to make sure the Viking ships were destroyed.

Emma looked angry. "You saved his life! He's a Viking!" she cried.

"Yes, I did," I told her calmly.

"He wanted to cut my throat! He wanted to hang me!" she said. She was so angry.

I smiled at her. "Yes, Emma. I know how that feels."

I turned my back on her and left her muttering words that my God would frown on.

My God said we must love our enemies. I put my arm around Ragnar's shoulder. "Come on, Ragnar – you're going to be a monk."

"But I'm a Viking," he said.

"Not any more," I told him. "You were the last Viking. The very last."

The True Story

The Vikings began raiding England on the 8th of June 793 AD, when they attacked a monastery on the north-east coast of England.

The people at the time said, "There were huge flashes of lightning, and fiery dragons were seen flying in the air."

The Viking raiders hacked some monks to death and dragged others into the sea to drown. They made others into slaves and robbed the monastery. For almost 300 years the Vikings brought nothing but terror to the Saxons in England.

But for a while the Vikings settled and their kings even became the rulers of England.

Then the Saxons were beaten by the Normans in 1066. Some Saxons tried to fight on. They asked their old enemies, the Vikings, for help against the Normans. They invited Hakkon to come back and rule.

In 1075 Hakkon's Vikings arrived and raided York. They were defeated. They never came back again. It was the last Viking raid on England. But they went on bringing terror to Ireland and Wales for many more years.

The real Symeon was a monk at Durham, and in the 11th century he wrote about the Viking raids. In 1075 he would have been a boy – and this could have been his story.

Viking Legends and Lies

Legend

The Vikings came to Britain in the year 787 AD. They landed with three boats on the south coast of England – in the Kingdom of Wessex. They were probably peaceful traders who wanted to buy and sell things. But they got into a fight and were driven off by the local people.

Lie

Some history books say the landing in 787 AD was the first Viking attack. That is silly. If the Vikings wanted to attack England they wouldn't have done it with just 3 boats and 50 men!

Legend

The Vikings returned to England in the year 793 AD when they attacked the monks on the island of Lindisfarne. Some monks were taken away as slaves and some were driven into the sea and drowned. The Vikings robbed the monastery and then sailed home with their loot.

Lie

Some history books say that the monks were so afraid that they prayed to God, "Please save us from the fury of the North Men" – the North Men were the Vikings. But this prayer was never spoken at the time. It was written hundreds of years later.

Legend

In the 9th century the Vikings began to leave their homes in Sweden, Denmark and Norway. They travelled all the way to Greenland and Iceland in the north. They discovered America in the west and raided Italy. No one is sure why they decided to change from being farmers to raiders.

Lie

Some history books say the Vikings used to raid in the summer, when the seas were calm, then go home in the winter. But by 850 AD the Vikings arrived at the River Thames and they stayed there. Maybe they really wanted to be farmers and traders, not raiders.

Legend

The Vikings could be fierce fighters. Some of them went wild in battle and were known as "Berserkers". They wore coats made of bear skin. "Berserk" means "bear shirt". The Vikings thought the bear skin gave them the strength of a bear.

Lie

Some history books say the Viking leader Ragnar was captured by King Ella of Northumbria and thrown into a pit of snakes. The Viking revenge was to capture Ella and rip out his lungs – the Blood Eagle torture. But the Blood Eagle was probably just a scary Viking story, not the truth.

Legend

In a sea battle the Vikings would try to ram their enemies' boats head-on. When the boats met, they would jump across and fight until one side won or they were all worn out. Sometimes they had to stop when the dead bodies were piled so high that the boat could no longer move forward.

Lie

Some history books say that the Vikings invented the longboat. But the oldest longboat ever found was not a Viking boat. It was built in Germany. It was built by the Jutes from Germany. They were using these longboats 400 years before the Vikings copied them and started their trading and raiding.

Legend

The Vikings were brave fighters but they were often beaten in battle. King Alfred smashed a Viking raid in Devon in the year 878 AD. Over 800 Vikings died and hardly any escaped. Then Alfred met a Viking army at Edington and beat them there too. The Vikings had to make peace with King Alfred.

Lie

Some history books say the word "Viking" means pirate. But that is probably not true. It may come from the Vikings' own word for "creek", where the Vikings launched their boats. Or it may come from the old English word that means "trader". No one will ever be sure.

Legend

The Vikings were not savages. At one
time England was ruled by the Viking King
Canute, and he was one of the best kings
England ever had. He built churches and
brought law and peace to England from
1016 AD.

Lie

Some history books say Viking leaders
were buried in longboats. But that did
not happen often. The boats cost far too
much money to be buried. Only a few of
the greatest Viking kings were buried in a
longboat.

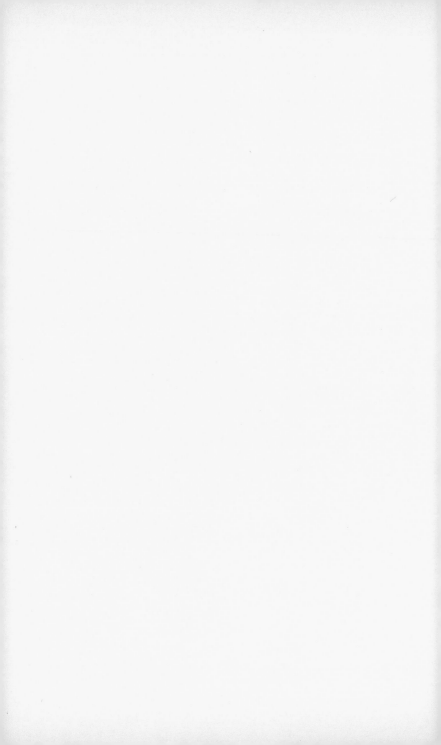

Our books are tested
for children and young people by
children and young people.

Thanks to everyone who consulted on
a manuscript for their time and effort in
helping us to make our books better
for our readers.

*Also by **Terry Deary** ...*

War Games

George is an evacuee from the Blitz. He has no friends and no family to turn to. At least he has cricket.

Esther is a Jewish girl in Nazi Germany. All her freedoms have been taken away. She cannot even play football.

Can a love of sport give two young people a way to survive?

Dick Turpin
Legends and Lies

7th April 1739. York. Today is the day Dick Turpin will die. A young boy waits in the crowd below the scaffold. Waits for a glimpse of the famous highwayman. Waits to see him hang.

In the crowd are five people – a villain, a victim, a fool, a traitor and an old man – who want to tell their stories. For some of them, the highwayman is a hero. For some of them, he is a monster.

Who is telling the truth?

www.barringtonstoke.co.uk